OUTER SPACE
STICKER BY NUMBER

How to Use This Book

There are so many surprises in outer space!

Look at the numbers and shapes in the white spaces. Then go to the front of the book to find the sticker with the matching color and shape. Place it on the blank space. Now you've completed the picture!

Try it with this planet!

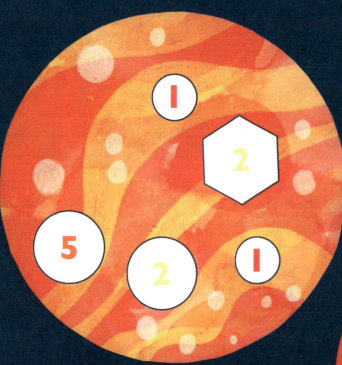

It should look like this picture after you find the correct stickers.

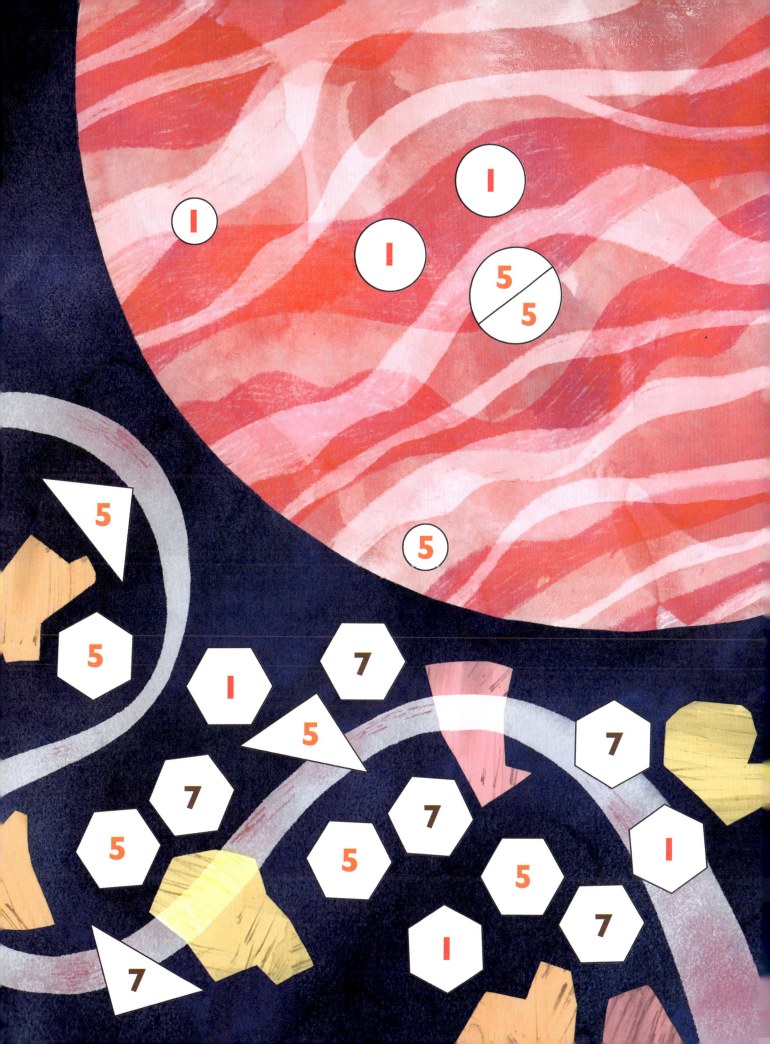

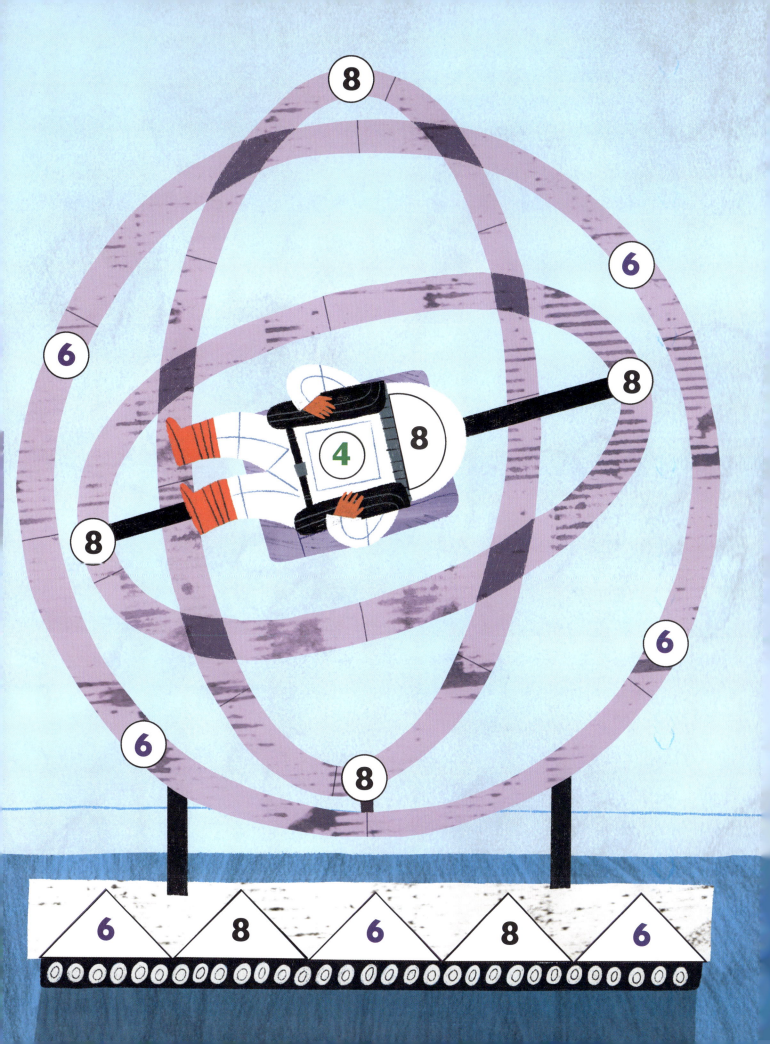

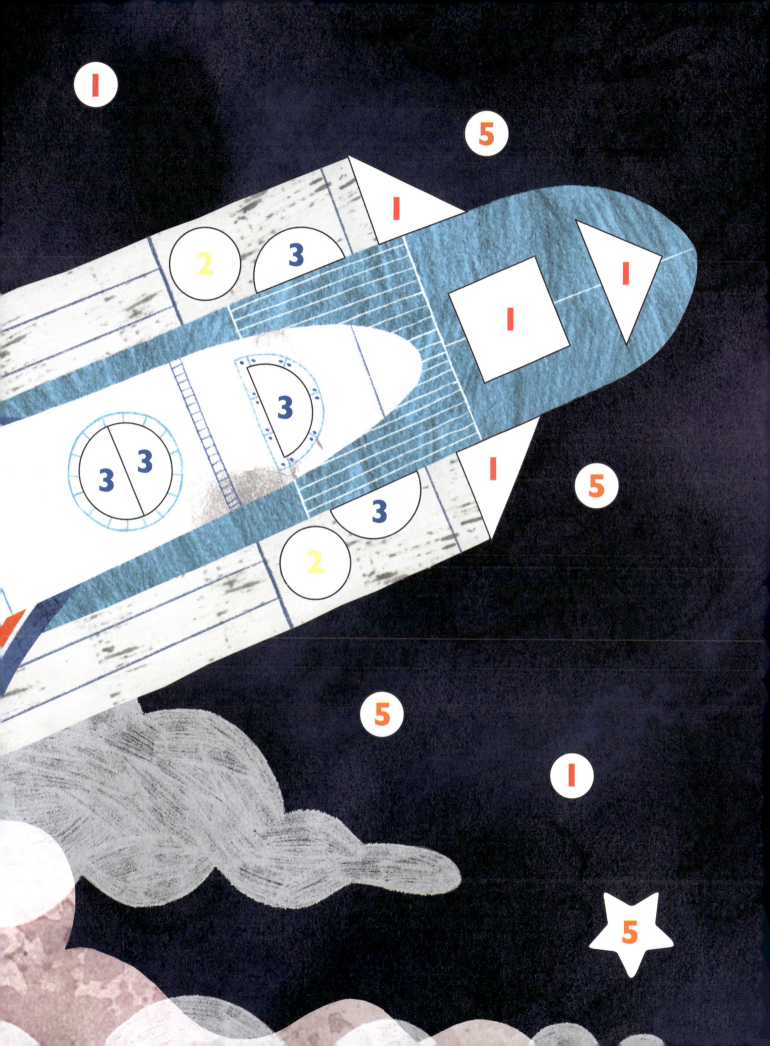

While in space, astronauts can also live at the International Space Station! It functions as a science lab for research too! Use your stickers to finish the ISS so that the busy astronauts can get to work!

The moon orbits around the Earth. Some planets have more than one moon orbiting them, but Earth just has one.

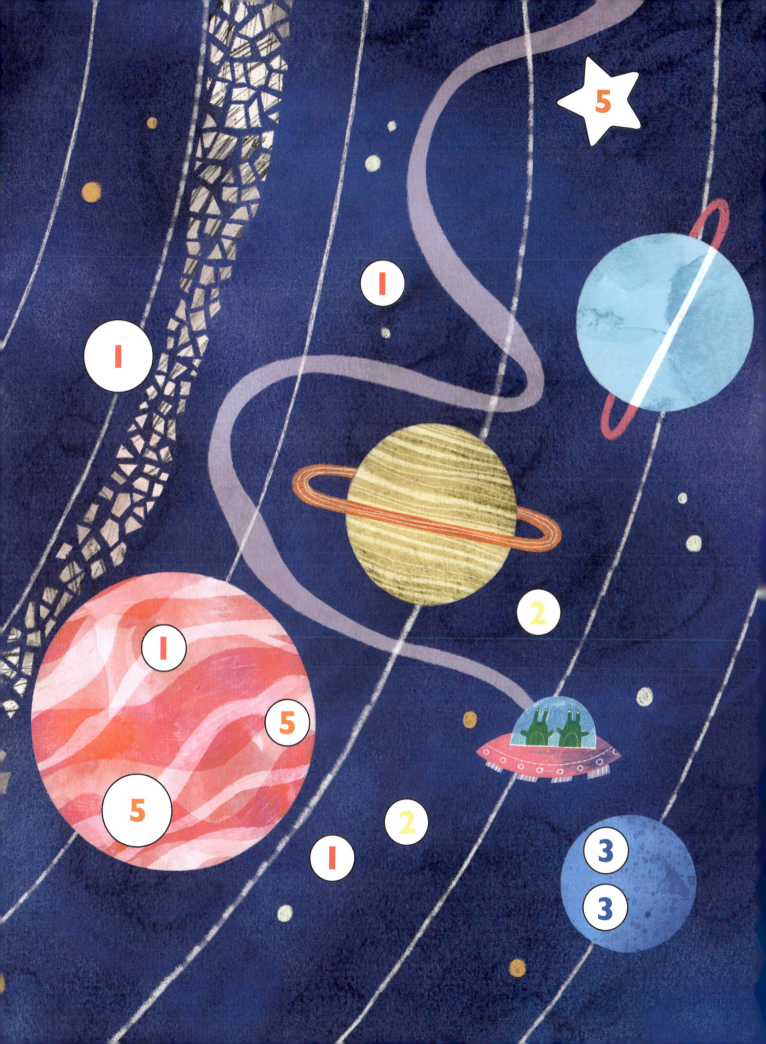